WALKING THROUGH THE JUNGLE

This edition is published by special arrangement with Orchard Books, New York.

Grateful acknowledgment is made to Orchard Books, New York, for permission to reprint *Walking Through the Jungle* by Debbie Harter.

Printed in the United States of America

ISBN 0-15-314502-1

18 175 2006

WALKING THROUGH THE JUNGLE

illustrated by Debbie Harter

Harcourt
Orlando Boston Dallas Chicago San Diego
www.harcourtschool.com

Walking through the jungle,
Walking through the jungle,

What do you see?
What do you see?

I think I see a lion,

Roar!

Roar!

Roar!

Chasing after me,
Chasing after me.

Floating on the ocean,
Floating on the ocean,

What do you see?
What do you see?

I think I see a whale,
Whoosh!
Whoosh!
Whoosh!

Chasing after me,
Chasing after me.

Climbing in the mountains,
Climbing in the mountains,

What do you see?
What do you see?

I think I see a wolf,
Howl!
Howl!
Howl!

Chasing after me,
Chasing after me.

Swimming in the river,
Swimming in the river,

What do you see?
What do you see?

I think I see a crocodile,
Snap!
Snap!
Snap!

Chasing after me,
Chasing after me.

Trekking in the desert,
Trekking in the desert,

What do you see?
What do you see?

I think I see a snake.
Hiss!
Hiss!
Hiss!

Chasing after me,
Chasing after me.

Slipping on the iceberg,
Slipping on the iceberg,

What do you see?
What do you see?

I think I see a polar bear,
Growl!
Growl!
Growl!

Chasing after me,
Chasing after me.

Running home for supper,
Running home for supper,

Where have you been?
Where have you been?

I've been around the world and back,
I've been around the world and back,

And guess what I've seen,
And guess what I've seen.